Goose on a roof

BY JENNIFER BARONE

ILLUSTRATIONS BY NATALIA STARIKOVA

To God, thank you for this wonderful gift. To my husband Luciano, my parents Agostino "Gus" and Linda. My brothers Fr. Vince, Jimmy, and my sister Rosalee who always helped me chase whatever dream I wanted to pursue. To my nephews and nieces Nicholas, Michael, Gregory, Lauren, Jaeden, Addison and Olivia. To the rest of my extended family and friends for their constant love and support.

"Believe in yourself and all that you are; know that there is something inside you that is greater than any obstacle." (Christian D Larson)

Goose On A Roof

Henry the goose lived on a beautiful farm down in the country. Henry was a quiet, small, friendly, and shy goose. The other geese were always mean to him and never accepted Henry as part of their flock.

"Hey Henry, you're not big, fast, or strong like us. We can fly high to the sky and over the barn through the meadow. You can't even fly over that wishing well! You will never be as tough as us," boasted Ronald the goose. Ronald was the strongest goose on the farm. He bullied Henry every time he came around.

1

Poor Henry walked away without saying a word. He walked very far across the barnyard and came across Farmer Gus' highest barn. Only the strongest geese could fly all the way up to its roof. Henry looked up but turned around and kept walking. It's no use, he thought to himself.

But then he thought "I CAN DO IT, I CAN
DO IT! I'll show those other geese!"

So Henry raised his wings and flapped as hard as
he could, but only flew up just a little bit.

The next time, Henry took 3 steps back, ran a little bit, and again
raised his wings and flapped and flapped as hard as he could.

"I CAN DO IT! I...I...I...I DID IT!"

Henry was so proud that he made it to the top of the barn.

"Wait until my friends see me up here. They will be so
proud of me!"

But when Henry looked down he suddenly didn't feel so well. That barn was so high, and Henry did not have the courage to get down from the roof. Hours and hours went by and Henry still couldn't move.

Along came Rocky the dog and yelled up at Henry. Rocky was a happy dog who loved to play fetch on the farm. He was Henry's best friend.

"Hey Henry, just fly down using your wings!"

"I can't Rocky," said Henry. "I'm too scared!"

Then along came Polly the cow. Polly was a delightful cow. She was very motherly to all the animals on the farm.

"Henry!" yelled Polly. "Use your wings!"

"Oh Polly, It's terrible. I can't, I don't remember how," wailed Henry.

7

Hearing all that racket, Paloma the horse trotted over. Paloma was a courageous horse who always helped Henry to persevere in being himself.

"Henry the goose, you start flapping those wings and you get down here this instant!" Henry started to sob. "I am stuck up here forever!"

At that moment Ronald the goose and all his friends were flying by the barn

"Ha ha ha, Henry the goose. We told you you're not strong and fast like us! You will never be as tough as us!"

Suddenly, Henry's sobs turned into angry words.

"Oh yeah! I CAN DO IT, I CAN DO IT, I CAN DO IT!" Henry closed his eyes, flapped his wings with all his might.

"I...I...I DID IT!"

When Henry opened his eyes he had made it back to the ground. All of Henry's friends cheered for him, except for Ronald and the other geese.

"But...but how?" stuttered Ronald.

"Oh Ronald," said Henry. "Thank you for not believing in me. You helped me to believe in myself, and that is all that matters."

THE END

About the Author

Jennifer was born and raised in Sault Ste. Marie, Ontario. She is a Registered Early Childhood Educator who loves working with children of all ages. She enjoys reading, exercising and spending time with her family. She resides in Sault Ste. Marie with her husband Luciano.

 **FriesenPress**

Suite 300 - 990 Fort St

Victoria, BC, Canada, V8V 3K2

www.friesenpress.com

ISBN

978-1-4602-5505-6 (Paperback)

978-1-4602-5506-3 (eBook)

1. *Juvenile Fiction, Animals, Ducks, Geese, Etc.*

Distributed to the trade by The Ingram Book Company

CPSIA information can be obtained
at www.ICGtesting.com
Printed in the USA
LVIC06n2058181116
513309LV00001B/1

* 9 7 8 1 4 6 0 2 5 5 0 5 6 *